MYRIAD BOOKS LIMITED
35 Bishopsthorpe Road, London SE26 4PA

First published by
Andersen Press
20 Vauxhall Bridge Road
London SW1V 2SA
www.andersenpress.co.uk

Text copyright © Hiawyn Oram
Illustrations copyright © Frédéric Joos

ISBN 1 904 736 78 5

Printed in China

Getting-to-Grandad Bears

written by Hiawyn Oram
with pictures by Frédéric Joos

Myriad Books

Big Bear and Baby Bear were in the train on their way to visit Grandad.

"Are we nearly there yet?" said Baby Bear.

"No, no!" said Big Bear. "It's a long way and takes a long time to get to Grandad's."

"Then what shall we do to make it go faster?" said Baby Bear.

"Have some sandwiches," said Big Bear.
So Baby Bear ate some sandwiches and when
they were finished she licked her paws slowly.

"Are we nearly there *now?*" she said.
"No, no!" said Big Bear. "Not even nearly."
"Then what else shall we do to make it go faster?" said Baby Bear.

"Colouring-in," said Big Bear.
So Baby Bear coloured in and
joined the dots and coloured in
some more and joined some
more dots.

When everything was coloured in and all the dots joined, she put the tops back on her pens slowly.

"Are we nearly there *now?*" she said.

"No, no!" said Big Bear. "Not even half way!"

"Then what ELSE shall we do to make it go faster?" said Baby Bear.

"Read a story," said Big Bear.
So Baby Bear climbed onto Big Bear's lap and Big Bear read and Baby Bear listened and so did everyone else in their compartment.

When the story was finished Baby Bear closed the book slowly.

"Are we nearly there NOW?" she said.

"Uh . . . just past half way," said Big Bear.

"Then what CAN we do to get there faster?" said Baby Bear.

"Sleep?" said Big Bear, yawning.

"Sleep!" cried Baby Bear. "Much too slow!"
Then she jumped off Big Bear's lap and ran up
the corridor . . .

and down again . . .

WITHDRAWN

and up again . . .

and down and up again . . .

and out of the way of two Big Dogs . . .

and up again . . . and down again . . . until a
Baby Rabbit popped up and asked if he could
join her.

And they ran together . . . up the corridor . . .

and down again . . .

and up into a corner to whisper their secrets . . .

and down again . . . and out of the way of a
bad-tempered Big Pig . . .

and up again . . . and down again . . . and up again . . .
until they ran slap bang into the conductor.

"Whoops!" he said. "Better get back to your seats . . .
because you know what? We're coming into the station!"

"See!" said Baby Bear running back to Big Bear.
"What?" said Big Bear, opening the eye she was dozing with. "Are we nearly there?"
"Not *nearly!*" said Baby Bear. "We're THERE!"

"Right here!" said Grandad coming in to help with the luggage and picking up Baby Bear and kissing her and hugging her. "Have you had a long journey?"

"Oh no!" said Baby Bear. "'Cos I kept on running so we got here FASTER!"